W9-BLL-444

EJ 12
GIRL HERO

First American Edition 2015
Kane Miller, A Division of EDC Publishing

First published by Scholastic Australia Pty Limited in 2010
This edition published under license from Scholastic Australia Pty Limited on behalf of Lemonfizz Media

For information contact:
Kane Miller, A Division of EDC Publishing
P.O. Box 470663
Tulsa, OK 74147-0663
www.kanemiller.com
www.edcpub.com
www.usbornebooksandmore.com

Library of Congress Control Number: 2014949837

Printed and bound in the United States of America
7 8 9 10 11 12 13 14 15 16

ISBN: 978-1-61067-381-5

HOT & COLD

SSNNH MCFRLN

T MM
NSPRTN ND CNSLTNT
WTH LV

It was Monday morning, a school day, but there was no way Emma Jacks could go to school. She needed a plan—ideally one that would keep her away from school for the whole week.

Could it be a stomachache? Yes, that might work and actually, now that she thought about it, her stomach was sore. Quite sore. In fact, Emma was almost positive that she would soon need serious medical attention, and possibly hospital treatment. At the very least, her sore stomach would mean

staying home from school and not having to deal with mean girl Nema.

"Come on, Emma, hurry up! We're going to be late," Emma's mom shouted, from down the hallway.

Emma was not confident that her mother would agree with her self-diagnosis. She often didn't, which was irritating, so Emma would have to be clever about how she handled it.

"Okay, Mom, I'm coming!" Emma ran down the hall. It would have been way too obvious to lie in bed groaning—it was much better to act as if she was desperate to get to school, only to be struck down with an illness. She bounced into the kitchen and sat down at the table. And then, just as she picked up her spoon, she put her plan into action. She doubled over and moaned loudly.

"What's wrong, Em?" asked her mom, only briefly glancing up from the paper. Emma thought her mom should have been paying more attention.

"I don't know...but all of a sudden...my stomach really...hurts," said Emma in her quiet-but-act-like-you're-really-trying-to-speak-louder voice. She thought the pauses were a particularly good touch.

"It's probably your appendix," announced her older brother Bob. "Mom, I don't think we should waste any time with doctors. Let's amputate immediately—from the neck down. I'll get the bread knife."

"Hilarious, Bob! But Mom, now…it's really sore and…I think…" said Emma, in an even quieter voice, as she worked up to announcing her own diagnosis and treatment suggestion that she'd better stay home.

"This is very strange, Em," her dad interrupted, as he came out of the bathroom next door. (Although it sounded more like "is berry orange stem" because he had a mouth full of toothpaste.)

"What?" said everyone but Mom.

"Pardon?" said Mom.

"Sorry." He ducked back into the bathroom, rinsed his mouth, came out and tried again. "Well, I was just remembering how we have seen this illness before. Let me think…it first struck last year on the first day of school, and then the night of the school concert and also on the day of the gymnastics meet…"

"Dad, it's not that sort of illness at all," said Emma, in a voice that sounded slightly too loud and irritated for someone with severe stomach pain.

Emma's plan was not going quite as well as she'd hoped. Her family knew her too well.

Even though they could be irritating at times, Emma knew she could always rely on her family. They didn't change and they didn't pretend to be anything else but themselves. Dad was always Dad, looking a bit serious but then playing rock music really loud; Mom was always Mom, looking more relaxed and then turning down Dad's music; and Bob was always Bob, if you could get him away from his laptop. Mom, Dad, Bob. M-O-M, spelled exactly the same backward and forward, D-A-D the same again and even B-O-B too. Emma thought you could trust people with names like that. Suddenly Emma's thoughts were interrupted by her mom.

"Come on, Em," said Mom, giving her a squeeze.

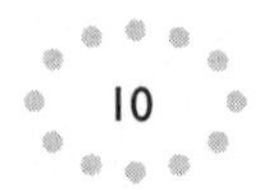

"You know that tummy will feel just fine once you get to school and if it doesn't, you can go to the nurse. Eat up now. We have to leave in ten minutes. And where did I leave my bag?"

Mom 1–Emma 0. Emma was left at the table, wondering what went wrong. She knew that look in her mom's eye—it was pointless to continue. She would just have to face up to Nema.

Emma and Nema had been at the same school all their lives and they had even been in the same kindergarten. They had organized sleepovers and been to all of each other's birthday parties. They weren't *best* friends, like Emma's friends Hannah and Elle were, but they were *good* friends. At least that's what Emma had thought. Then near the end of second grade, things had started to change for the worse. Nema got bossy, Nema got loud and

Nema got mean. *She was sneaky mean*, thought Emma. *Tricky mean—the kind of mean teachers never seem to see—the really* mean *mean.*

Nema had changed and Emma didn't like the new Nema nearly as much. Emma was pretty sure that *she* was still the same, but Nema blew hot and cold. One minute she was the nice Nema, chatting and laughing with Emma, and the next minute she would look right through her, or worse. She would say mean things, talk about Emma behind her back, or make fun of something Emma liked.

Like the time Nema and some other girls were dancing in the classroom at lunchtime. The music they were playing was the latest song by the Pink Shadows and it really made Emma want to dance. Emma and Elle asked if they could join in. But Nema said no.

"You'll never learn the moves, Emma. You'll just hold us up and we want to perform it in class tomorrow."

"It doesn't look that hard," Emma had replied.

"Well it is, so sorry, you can't," Nema had said.

"Who made you the boss, Nema?" Emma had asked.

"I did," Nema had snapped back. "And it's my CD. Do you have a problem with that?"

Emma had wanted to say yes, she did have a problem. But with Nema staring her down, she had felt like she was melting away. In fact, every time Emma was about to stand up to Nema, she seemed to melt away.

There was the time in third grade when Nema stopped everyone playing chase so they could watch her new gymnastics routine. No one knew why they should, but no one knew quite what to say either. Or the time when Nema took down other people's poster projects in the art room so her own project could go in the center. Again, everyone was so surprised they just let it happen.

So at least it wasn't just Emma. Nema seemed to boss everyone around and everyone seemed to let her get away with it. *Why was that?* Emma

thought. And now there was Nema's birthday party to deal with.

Nema was having a party and she was making sure that everyone knew about it. Obviously it was going to be "the best party this year" and "not a silly little girls' party" but a "real party." Nema and her friends would be "dressing to thrill." They would be picked up in a stretch limousine (complete with a television and mocktails) and taken to see a movie in a special cinema with big seats and party food to eat during the show.

"It will be fabulous, just awesome," said Nema to no one in particular in a whole group of girls outside

the lockers. "But you know, it's really special and really expensive, so only a select group can come. I don't know how I'm going to choose from all my friends!"

Emma couldn't believe what she was hearing. Nema was talking about her party in front of everyone —when everyone knew that you were supposed to keep quiet about parties that not everyone was invited to. *Everyone except Nema*, Emma thought to herself. She was pretty sure she could guess who had been invited.

There was a group of girls who were always buzzing around Nema, giggling at everything she said and following her around—they would be on the list for sure. *But who else?* Emma couldn't imagine, so she nearly fell over when she received an invitation too. She didn't think she and Nema were friends anymore. *Why is Nema asking me—and what will the party be like with all those giggly girls?* She also wondered who else might have received an unexpected invitation. *If I'm invited, then surely*

Elle and Hannah will be too. That might be okay—it might even be fun!

But it wasn't okay and it certainly wasn't fun. The morning after Emma received her invitation, all the girls were hanging around their lockers waiting for class to start.

"Hey, Elle!" shouted Nema. "Did you get the invitation to my party?"

"No." Elle turned around with surprise.

"Oh, that's right," said Nema sweetly. "I forgot—I didn't invite you! Why would I? You probably wouldn't be able to see the movie with those glasses on."

There was a hush and then the girls around Nema giggled and Emma watched as her friend's face turned red and her eyes blinked hard.

Elle isn't going? Well, who else is *going*, she thought, and why would Nema be so mean about it? *Why would anyone say something like that? And in front of everyone too!* She thought Elle's new glasses were totally cool, but she knew that Elle was still feeling funny about having to wear them.

"Nema..." Emma started. She wanted to tell Nema that what she had said was really mean. She wanted to tell her that you shouldn't treat people that way. She wanted to...

"Yes, Emz?" asked Nema innocently. "I do hope *you* can come. It will be great having all the popular girls together."

"But Nema, you can't..." Emma felt her voice melt away.

"I can't what?" Nema's voice suddenly changed. It was sharp and icy cold. "What can't I do, Emma? I can't talk? But I *am* talking, listen to me!"

The other girls with Nema giggled.

"Nema, you can't..." Emma tried again.

"What, Emma? Has the cat got your tongue? Anyway, let me know about the party by Monday or you won't be able to come either. I have to confirm the final numbers. Come on, girls, we're out of here!"

Nema and the girls flounced off, chatting as they wandered down the corridor. Elle looked crushed and embarrassed and Emma felt awful. She should have stood up for her friend. She had let Elle down. But it was so hard to be brave and say the right things when Nema was so mean. In fact, Emma found it difficult to say anything at all.

"Elle, I'm so sorry, I should have stood up for you," she said to her friend.

"It doesn't matter. Who cares what Nema thinks?" said Elle, but she didn't look as if she believed it.

"We don't! But what she said to you was so mean, Elle," Emma replied. She put a comforting arm around her friend, who still looked as if she might burst into tears. "And so untrue—your glasses are cool. I bet Nema's secretly jealous!"

"Maybe," said Elle quietly. "But it doesn't matter. Em, did Nema really invite you to the party?"

"Yes, but I don't know why. Her mom probably made her because we're still on the same gymnastics team. We're not really good friends anymore."

"Em! You're not going to go, are you?"

"Um..." Emma didn't know what to say. She hadn't expected to be invited, but she thought that the limousine ride and the special cinema might be fun. But now that she knew that her other friends weren't going, she wasn't so sure.

"Emma, you're not really thinking about it, are you?" Elle raised her eyebrows.

"Um, well, no, I don't think so...but she *did* ask me and I don't want to..."

"You don't want to what? Upset Nema? Would you rather go to a party wearing silly dresses, makeup and movie star hair—which you hate—with a whole lot of girls who are mean?" Elle was starting to sound a little annoyed.

"No, but Elle, maybe..."

And then the bell went and Emma had gymnastics practice straight after school so she didn't get to finish talking to Elle. And then it was the weekend and she couldn't talk to Elle because her whole family was away at a wedding.

Emma felt bad. First she had felt bad for not sticking up for Elle when Nema was mean, and then Elle made her feel bad for thinking she might go to the party.

Is it bad to think about going to the party? Is that a bit like not sticking up for my friend? Does Elle think I'm mean now too? And what will Nema say if I say I'm not going? What will Elle say if I go? Which is worse—Aaaaaaaaaaargh! Emma couldn't think straight anymore, but she knew one thing—she really wished she had never been invited to the party.

And then, much too soon, it was Monday. She had to let Nema know whether she was going to the party. And what was she going to do now that her cunning "too sick to go to school" plan had failed?

Only one thing could save her now—a mission alert from SHINE.

Chapter 3

Emma Jacks, average ten-year-old girl, was also EJ12—a field agent and ace code-cracker in the under-twelve division of **SHINE**, a secret agency that protected the world from evildoers. And while Emma Jacks often found it hard to deal with mean girls, irritating brothers and other everyday problems, EJ12 was unbeatable. Compared to dealing with mean girls at school, saving the world was easy!

Emma hadn't planned on being a spy. It just sort of happened. There had been an elementary school math competition and Emma's school was competing. Emma was beyond excited about the competition. She loved math and she loved solving problems. When she found out she had won, she was beyond whatever beyond excited is.

She had imagined receiving a certificate and maybe even a medal, which might be presented at a school assembly. Everyone would be clapping, her friends would be cheering and Emma would feel a little bit embarrassed, act *completely* embarrassed, but secretly quite enjoy the fuss. She knew her parents would go on and on about how proud they were and even Bob would mumble something that she would take as a compliment. She would quite like that as well.

Emma had never imagined that she and her mom would be picked up from home in a large black car with dark windows that would take them to a shop—a lighting shop of all places. Feeling a little surprised, she had followed her mom into the shop and told the woman at the counter who they were.

"Oh yes, Emma, we've heard all about you. Congratulations!" said the shopkeeper.

Emma couldn't think why a lady running a lighting shop would have heard about her, let alone congratulate her, but she didn't say anything.

"And welcome! Just take the elevator on your right and press the button with the lightbulb on it," the shopkeeper said, smiling.

Welcome to what? Emma thought this was weird, but her mom didn't seem too surprised.

"Maybe math people just do things that way," she grinned.

Emma didn't think that was a very good explanation. She entered the elevator, held the doors open for her mom, then pressed the lightbulb button and waited. The elevator jolted and began to go down . . . down, down and then down some more—twenty floors down in fact. And then the elevator stopped, the door opened, and Emma found herself standing in front of an oldish lady with long white hair whipped up into a slightly messy bun with a few pencils sticking out of it.

"Welcome to **SHINE**, Emma Jacks. I'm A1."

"To SHINE?" said Emma. "But I'm supposed to be picking up my math prize."

"And so you are, Emma, but maybe it's not the prize you were expecting. SHINE is an underground agency," A1 explained.

"Well I know that," said Emma. "We just came down twenty floors in the elevator."

"No, Emma," smiled A1. "I mean it's a secret agency. Mrs. Jacks, would you like to take a seat in our lounge area while I explain SHINE to Emma?"

"How lovely," replied Emma's mom.

Emma thought her mom should have said something else. Something like, "Perhaps I'll just stay here and see what happens to my daughter twenty floors below street level in a secret organization!" But no, she didn't. And strangely enough, Emma didn't really mind. She could tell immediately that A1 was someone she could trust.

"Come with me, Emma. I'll show you around," said A1. She pushed a button and a door that Emma hadn't even noticed slid open to reveal a large room filled with desks and an enormous flat screen flashing images and numbers in the middle of them. Everywhere Emma looked there were women sitting at the desks, working in front of screens, talking on headsets and typing furiously on keyboards.

"What is this? What is everyone doing?" asked Emma.

"Solving problems," said A1 in a serious voice, "and stopping evil plans. And you can help us, Emma. The math competition you won was our way of recruiting new agents. We need clever thinkers, especially people who love math, and it doesn't matter how old they are. We need agents to help us crack enemy codes and thwart the evil missions of the *SHADOW* agency. We defeat *SHADOW*," A1 explained, "by intercepting their secret messages, getting to their locations before their own agents and foiling their dastardly plans."

"That all sounds rather dangerous," said Emma quietly.

"Let danger be a stranger!" declared A1 heartily.

"That's one of SHINE's mottoes—we like mottoes. We also know our agents well and we know what they can do—sometimes even before they do. SHINE needs you, Emma. We have run a complete check on you and you are exactly what we need for our under-twelve division."

"I think maybe the results got mixed up," suggested Emma nervously.

"We never get our results mixed up," said A1, suddenly looking slightly less friendly and slightly more scary. "You are exactly what SHINE needs. Everything is organized. Your training has been set up and you are ready to go. But the one thing that you must remember above all else is that your job is top secret—only classified people can be informed about your activities."

"But what about Mom?" asked Emma.

"Don't worry about your mother," said A1 with a wink. "We know exactly how to deal with mothers."

Well, thought Emma, *if they can handle moms, they must be pretty special.*

And so it began. Emma Jacks became EJ12, Class A field agent and code-cracker, under-twelve division, for SHINE. Since that day, EJ12—or just EJ, as she was called when she was on duty—had foiled evil plans all over the world. She had jumped out of planes, dived into oceans and climbed mountains. She had cracked some of the trickiest codes around and beaten *SHADOW* time after time. In fact, EJ12 had quickly become one of SHINE's Shining Stars, a leader in the agency's Spy of the Year competition.

The funny thing was, while Emma Jacks often worried about normal everyday things, EJ12 seemed to be able to handle anything on a mission. *Why was that?* Emma really wished she knew. And sometimes she really wished EJ12 could come along to school in her place, just to sort everything out.

But she couldn't. It was quarter past eight, there was no mission alert from SHINE and there was nothing for it—Emma Jacks was going to school.

Chapter 4

It was just Mom and Emma in the car, as Bob had already left for soccer practice. Emma could feel a "talk" coming on. Her hunch was right. They had barely pulled out of the driveway when her mom started.

"What's *really* going on, Em?" she said. "You've been out of sorts all weekend."

"Nothing," Emma mumbled. "I just had—I mean have—a really sore stomach…"

"Really, Em, I know that tummy," said Mom, as she turned off the car radio.

Uh-oh. Emma knew what that meant—Mom definitely wanted to talk and she wasn't going to be distracted. Actually, Emma didn't mind so much. She quite liked talking to her mom, even if she did go on a bit.

"Is it something at school?"

"Sort of, yes. I hate school! Please can I stay home, just today, just this once?" Emma pleaded.

"Well, where's all this coming from? Is it something to do with your class or your friends?"

"Sort of both," Emma squirmed.

"Em! Is it someone or something?" Now Mom had her.

"It's someone," Emma said quietly.

"Come on then, what's happening, little one?"

Emma hated it if her mom called her "little one" when there were other people around, but she loved it when it was just the family. It made her feel safe and protected, like a little girl—a little girl who didn't have to deal with *mean* girls. Suddenly Emma felt teary. Her face reddened and the words rushed out.

"Oh Mom, it's awful. It's Nema. She's so mean —mean to me, mean to Elle, mean to Hannah, mean to everyone. And now she's invited me to her movie party, but she hasn't invited Elle and Elle doesn't think I should go, and I probably don't think I should go and I don't even want to go, but I didn't say that and now Elle probably thinks I'm mean too, and today is the day I have to say if I'm going to the party, and what if I say no and Nema is mean to me and then ..."

Emma ran out of breath so her mom jumped in. "But I thought you and Nema were friends?"

"We used to be, and sometimes we still are, but mostly now she just wants to do hairstyles and dance routines—and make fun of everyone who doesn't."

"Can't you just play with some of your other friends?" Mom suggested, trying to be helpful.

"But Mom, it's not that easy. Nema's everywhere. She breaks up games and tries to be the boss of everything. She's so mean that most people just give in so that she'll stop being horrible. And of course, that just makes her worse. And what will I do about the party?"

"What do *you* think you should do?" asked Mom.

"I probably shouldn't go."

"Then just say, 'thanks a lot, but I can't go,'" Mom smiled.

Aaaaaaaaaaaaaargh! Emma knew her mom was really trying, but she just didn't get it. If someone said something to Nema that she didn't like, then Nema would say something really mean back. She would stare at you, daring you to say something, and if you did come up with something she would flick her hair, raise her eyebrows and say, "Whatever. Who cares what you think?" And then no one felt brave and everyone went quiet and Nema would win. Again.

"I'm not sure that's a good idea," said Emma.

"Oh, Em, it won't be as hard as you think," said Mom, as they pulled up on the street outside the school. "Off you go. Love you!"

As her mom drove off, Emma took a quick, hopeful look at her phone. *Nothing*. Oh well, at least she had a phone, she thought, even if it wasn't flashing. Before joining SHINE, she didn't have a mobile phone at all.

"Let's talk about it again next year," Mom had said, and mobile phones looked set to join the growing list of things that Emma and her mom were going to discuss when she was older: pierced ears, more pocket money, getting a puppy and using online chat rooms. Emma and her mom were going to be talking a lot.

But when Emma had received a really cool phone as part of her new agent welcome pack, after her visit to the SHINE lighting shop, her mom had agreed she could keep it. This was rather unexpected, but Emma put it down to A1's mother-management skills, and she certainly wasn't about to complain.

Emma's stomach did a little backflip as she turned into school. *Please, please let me see Hannah or Elle before I see Nema. Please let me see Louisa or Grace or Catherine before I see Nema. Please let me see Isi or even Madison—or anyone else before I see Nema!*

But there was Nema, hanging around in the corridor near the lockers. Emma couldn't possibly get past without Nema noticing her. And then she would ask Emma about the party...

Piinngg!

EJ reached for her phone and was relieved to see the screen flashing, a nice aqua, aqua being Emma's favorite color and the color for the SHINE mission alert. *Saved by the flash! At last*, thought Emma. *Something is going my way.*

"Hey, Emma," cried Nema. "Where are you going? We need to talk about the party."

"Um, sorry," called Emma, as she skipped down the corridor. "I have to go to the bathroom."

"Gross," said Nema, wrinkling up her face. "Too much information!"

If only you knew, thought Emma, hurrying toward the girls' bathroom with a grin.

Chapter 5

Once inside the girls' bathroom, Emma turned on the hand dryers, headed for the last stall on the right and pushed the door.

"Hey," cried a voice from behind the stall door. "I'm in here!"

"Oh, sorry," replied Emma. "No problem, take your time."

Emma waited, feeling slightly fidgety. She needed to get to the Mission Tube—quickly. The Mission Tube was the secret network that took

SHINE agents to the Code Room and then on to SHINE HQ for mission briefings. It was very clever—and very fun—but Emma wished it didn't have to start in the bathroom. It was a bit gross.

The toilet flushed and then an older girl came out. *At last!*

"Thanks!" said Emma.

"What's wrong with the other six stalls?" asked the girl. "They're all empty."

"Yes, but...but..." *But what?* "But I like this one."

Groan.

"Er, okay," said the girl, looking at Emma as if she was a bit strange. "Whatever."

Whatever indeed! Emma rushed into the stall and locked the door. She put down the toilet seat, sat down and flipped open the toilet paper holder—and Mission Tube access pad. Emma pushed her mobile phone into a small socket on the side of the toilet paper holder and waited. There was a beep, then Emma entered her pin code and removed her phone. Another beep and then the usual message flashed up on her phone screen.

WELCOME BACK EJ12.
HOLD ON!

EJ loved what was coming next. She held on to the edge of the toilet seat in preparation. Suddenly, the wall behind the toilet spun around, with the toilet and EJ still attached. EJ slipped off the toilet seat and onto a beanbag at the top of a giant tunnel slide. A protective shield lowered itself down and clicked into place over the beanbag. EJ was about to enter the SHINE Mission Tube. The wall spun back and EJ could hear the click as the stall door unlocked. No one would ever guess she'd been in there. EJ typed "go" into her phone...

WHOOSH!

EJ slid down a giant pipe, shiny and brightly lit, just one of the many secret underground tubes in the SHINE network. It was like a toboggan ride with no snow and a beanbag instead of a toboggan. EJ giggled as she whizzed through the pipe, but all too soon it was over and she stopped at a small platform with a keypad. First stop—the Code Room. A code-cracking room. If the agents cracked the code before they arrived at SHINE HQ, it gave SHINE time to read the decoded message and help prepare the mission briefing. That meant the agent could get going quicker on her mission. It was clever, but then SHINE was clever, very bright. EJ flipped back the protective shield of the keypad, keyed in her pin code and waited for the security check.

The check changed each time EJ arrived at the Code Room. Sometimes it was fingerprints, sometimes eye scans or voice recognition. You never knew what it would be—and neither did anyone trying to break into the SHINE network.

"Stand up and look straight ahead. Then poke your tongue out," requested a digital voice.

EJ grinned. *Tongue scan—very mature.* As she poked out her tongue, there was a short sharp flash.

"Tongue scan complete. Agent identity confirmed. Please drop in, EJ12."

There was another beep, then EJ did exactly that. The floor underneath opened and both EJ and the beanbag dropped gently down into a small chamber. EJ had entered the Code Room, a small room with nothing in it except a table and chair and, above the table, a clear plastic tube protruding from the ceiling. Keeping her eyes on the tube, EJ sat and waited. She knew what would happen next, and soon enough she heard the familiar whizzing noise. She cupped her hands, put them under the tube and caught a little capsule that popped out of the tube. It was the code capsule.

EJ opened it and took out a small piece of paper and a little pencil. She could feel the butterflies starting to flutter inside her. She always felt a little nervous opening the code, but it was a good, excited nervous as she got ready to crack the code. It was a little like waiting for a race to start. EJ unfolded the paper. It felt crisp and clean between her fingers. EJ smiled with anticipation as she read.

For the eyes of EJ12 only.

(intercepted message)

VLPL PP S PRFCTD ND PLR TP

RDY FR BSNSS.

PY PRMPTLY T MPRR PNGN

PNT FR PRVW ND PRTY NVTTN.

PYMNT: 20 MLLN DLLRS BY MDDY

PRTY: DRSS T CHLL WTH

DR C HLL 6PM

Codes, EJ just loved them. They were confusing at first because they looked like one thing and then turned out to be something else—a bit like Nema really. But once you understood how they worked, they were easy to handle. She wished Nema was like that too. *If only I could crack the Nema code!*

Back to the code, she thought and then smiled as she looked at it carefully. *This has to be the easiest code yet. It looks more like a text message than a code. Or should that be a txt mssg?* EJ remembered one of the main rules of code-cracking in her agent training. *Look for what's there—or for what's missing. And what's missing here is the vowels. Too easy!* She had decoded the message in no time at all.

For the eyes of EJ12 only.

(intercepted message)

VLPL PP S PRFCTD ND PLR TP
VLPL PIPE IS PERFECTED AND POLAR TAP
RDY FR BSNSS.
READY FOR BUSINESS.
PY PRMPTLY T MPRR PNGN
PAY PROMPTLY AT EMPEROR PENGUIN
PNT FR PRVW ND PRTY NVTTN.
POINT FOR PREVIEW AND PARTY INVITATION.
PYMNT: 20 MLLN DLLRS BY MDDY
PAYMENT: 20 MILLION DOLLARS BY MIDDAY
PRTY: DRSS T CHLL WTH
PARTY: DRESS TO CHILL WITH
DR C HLL 6PM
DR C HILL 6PM

Well, nearly all the code. Everything except the first word. EJ couldn't work out what letters could be missing from VLPL. VALPAL? VELPAL? VULPAL? Nothing seemed to make sense, to make a real word.

The rest of the code was not much better: it was one thing to crack the code, but it was quite another to understand what the decoded message meant. Some messages were actually much more puzzling than the codes.

EJ frowned, as she often did when she was thinking hard. She was still frowning and thinking as she folded the paper, put it back in the capsule and put the capsule back into the tube. Within seconds, it was sucked up and away, on its way to SHINE HQ.

And I'd better get there quick-smart too, thought EJ12. It was time for the mission briefing.

Chapter 6

After another trip on the Mission Tube, EJ was at SHINE HQ. And, as always, A1 was standing there ready to greet her.

"Good to see you, EJ12. Things are really hotting up. The message we intercepted—and the code you have just cracked—is an important breakthrough."

"What do you mean, A1?"

"For the last few months, we have suspected that something was happening at a polar ice cap. But up until now we didn't know *what*, we didn't know *which* polar cap—the south or the north—and we didn't know *who*. Now, thanks to you, we know all of those things."

"Um, *what* do we know?" asked EJ, feeling slightly bewildered by A1's whats, whichs and whos.

"Ah, it's more a case of *what* we still don't know," sighed A1. "We know *where* and *who* but not *what* or *why*. And now that I think of it, we don't know *when* either!"

"I'm not sure I know *what* you're talking about," replied EJ.

"But of course, I'm rushing ahead," smiled A1. "Let's go back to the decoded message." A1 turned to look at the ceiling. "Light Screen lower. Show code."

EJ loved the Light Screen. It was kind of like the **SHINE** brain—a giant, voice-activated plasma screen that accessed the Internet, all **SHINE**'s classified files, radio and television channels and GPS technology too. *If only I could have a light screen at home,* thought EJ. *It's so much better than any ordinary computer. Very cool.* The decoded message that EJ had just cracked flashed on to the screen.

INTERCEPTED CODE
CRACKED BY AGENT EJ12 0835

VLPL PIPE IS PERFECTED AND POLAR TAP
READY FOR BUSINESS.
PAY PROMPTLY AT EMPEROR PENGUIN POINT
FOR PREVIEW AND PARTY INVITATION.
PAYMENT: 20 MILLION DOLLARS BY MIDDAY

PARTY: DRESS TO CHILL WITH
DR C HILL 6PM

"Okay, so what do we know now?" said A1.

"We know someone likes the letter P?" said EJ.

"Yes, indeed EJ, but we also know that there is some kind of pipe called something like the Velpil or Volpal Pipe and it is connected to something called a Polar Tap. We know Dr. C. Hill is behind it and, because we intercepted this message on its way to ***SHADOW***, we also know that ***SHADOW*** is the customer."

"But who is Dr. C. Hill?" asked EJ.

"Ah, Dr. C. Hill, we know her well," said A1 quietly. "Profile Caterina Hill."

A picture of a woman appeared on the Light Screen. She was beautiful but in a pointy, cold, unsmiling kind of way. With straight blonde, almost white hair, Dr. Hill had a long, narrow face and small lips with a slash of blood-red lipstick across them. Her eyes were black and her eyebrows arched in a thin jet-black line. She was wearing a white laboratory coat with a foxtail cape draped over her shoulders, and EJ was fairly sure it was not fake fur. Her fingers were long with black painted nails.

"Meet Dr. C. Hill," said A1.

"I think I'd rather not," said EJ.

"She does look a bit threatening, doesn't she?" agreed A1. "Glamorous I suppose, but I can't imagine how she gets anything done with nails like that."

EJ glanced at A1's nails and they were exactly as she expected—short, neat, clean, no polish. No-nonsense nails.

"However," A1 continued, "Dr. Hill is one of the world's cleverest scientists and inventors. In fact, she used to work here at SHINE, leading the way in temperature control and inventing ingenious ways to use natural hot and cold power sources. Indeed, she had been working on a number of top secret projects that could have done wonderful things for the world. She was experimenting with using the heat in volcanoes to make energy and was testing ways to freeze water. These things could help slow the effects of global warming. Can you imagine how that could have changed things, EJ? But then, just as it seemed she had made an important breakthrough, she disappeared."

"Where? Why?" asked EJ, enthralled by the story of this fierce-looking woman. "What went wrong?"

"She became greedy, I think," sighed A1. "She wanted more and more money and more and more control. She was becoming impossible to work with, always needing to be the one in charge, and would not listen to anyone else. She insisted on working alone, never sharing any results or information. You're too young to know this, but there are some very mean people in this world."

"Oh, I think I'm old enough to understand," said EJ.

"Caterina spiraled out of control," continued A1. "She demanded ten million dollars for her latest invention. We had to say no and she was furious. You could say she had a complete meltdown." A1 paused and chuckled at her own joke. "The next day, she simply disappeared—taking her entire laboratory with her."

"Where did she go?"

"Up until now we weren't sure, but this message solves that little mystery. She's invented the Pipe, which has something to do with a Polar Tap—and ***SHADOW*** wants to buy it. And I see the price has now doubled—she's asking for twenty million dollars! And if ***SHADOW*** is in the market for it, then you can bet it is not good."

EJ nodded in agreement.

"This message also makes sense of other information we have been collecting in the area. Watch the screen, EJ." A1 turned to look at the screen again. "Show charts," she said. A whole lot of graphs appeared on the Light Screen, many of them flashing red. "As you can see, EJ, in the region of the South Pole, where she is, we have been recording very strange temperatures and water level increases lately. They are much, much hotter and much, much higher than they should be, even allowing for global warming. Something or someone is causing the polar temperatures to rise and, if I'm not mistaken, that someone is Dr. Caterina Hill."

"But how do you know she's at the *South* Pole?" said EJ.

"Penguins"

"Pardon?"

"Penguins." A1 smiled. "Emperor Penguin Point. Emperor penguins are only found at the South Pole. So she has to be there."

EJ knew her geography pretty well—well enough to know that the South Pole was huge. Searching for someone there would be like trying to find a snowflake in a blizzard.

"I know what you're thinking, EJ. How will we ever find Caterina in all that white wilderness?"

EJ's eyes widened. *How does A1 always do that?* She seemed to be able to read EJ's mind.

"But look closely at the message, there's another clue," A1 explained.

"Emperor Penguin Point?"

"Exactly," nodded A1. "Emperor penguins are only found in a few areas on Antarctica and one of their largest breeding grounds is on a small island off the ice shelf and off the mainland of Antarctica. Our satellite photos show there is also an abandoned research hut there. That means there's a pretty good chance it's the drop-off point for the payment. However, if you do your job, EJ, it will be *Caterina* who is caught out in the cold when you, and not a **SHADOW** agent, make the payment and turn up as the special guest."

Great, thought EJ. *Now I have two invitations to parties I really don't want to go to.*

Chapter 7

EJ thought hard. There was so much information to absorb. "But A1," she said. "Surely we're not going to give Dr. Hill twenty million dollars?"

"Only temporarily, EJ, don't worry," explained A1. "We will freeze the account once you have located Caterina and shut down her operation."

"And what do I do if I run into Dr. Hill?" asked EJ.

"We're hoping you *do* run into her, EJ12. We need to put a stop to all her evil plotting. You will know what to do," said A1 mysteriously. "Our agents always do. And don't forget one of our favorite mottoes: 'We stand up when others let you down.' And you, EJ12, you can stand up to anyone." A1 smiled.

If only you knew, thought EJ sadly. She had already let down Elle this week. What if she let down A1 and **SHINE** as well?

"No time for daydreaming, EJ. We need to get you on your way."

A1 was right, of course. The clock was already ticking.

"You are going to the coldest and windiest region on Earth, so your gear is very important," continued A1.

EJ looked toward the briefing table where all her mission gear was laid out waiting for her: thick waterproof ski pants, a padded jacket with a furry hood (fake fur of course), ski goggles, gloves and boots.

"Take special note of your boots, EJ. They might look like ordinary mission boots, but the soles can change to allow you to travel on any surface. Simply click the heels together to activate them. There are several different options, so click through until you find the one you need."

That was smart—and very spy-like. But EJ had also seen something else very cool at the end of the table. It was a bracelet with charms attached: a little silver penguin, an ice pick, a heart, a boat and a little key. She was hoping the bracelet was part of her kit, but could not see how it was going to be.

A1 must have been reading her mind, again!

"Yes, it's yours, EJ, but this is no ordinary bracelet. We have been trying to develop a way for our agents to carry their tools without attracting attention, and we think we may have succeeded with this little item. Each charm is actually a piece of equipment —you twist it to activate its special properties. The key is a standard SHINE skeleton key. Twist it and it will extend to fit any lock. There's no time now to go through them all, but they may prove useful."

Suddenly EJ spied a metallic-aqua touch screen phone on the lab bench next to her clothes. "Um, is that for this mission as well?" she asked hopefully, pointing at the phone.

"Absolutely, EJ. I nearly forgot," replied A1. "Your phone needs an upgrade. You need a model that has satellite reception—there's no mobile phone reception where you're heading. This one also works as a games console in case you need to disguise the phone. There are lots of other applications, or apps, that may come in handy, and I think we got the color right as well, didn't we?"

"Yes, thanks, A1," smiled EJ, handing over her old phone and pocketing the new one.

"Okay then," finished A1. "Now we need to make that payment deadline. Agent X1 is waiting for you at SHINE docks with *Microlight*. She will take you out to the icebreaker where you will receive your full mission briefing. Good luck, EJ12, and smooth sailing—or should that be smooth speeding?"

Speeding was definitely the better word. *Microlight* was one of SHINE's supersonic speedboats. While it was small—just big enough for two people—its special engine made it superfast, which was just as well because they were speeding toward the polar ice cap, a journey that would normally take days. It also made it super fun—EJ had to admit there were definite advantages to being a SHINE agent.

As the little boat jumped wave after wave, the wind raced through EJ's hair and salt spray sprinkled her face. After a while, EJ noticed that little chunks of ice were starting to appear in the water.

"Not long now," shouted X1, as she jumped the boat into another wave. "In fact, look over there to your left!"

As EJ turned, she saw an enormous shape appear on the horizon. As *Microlight* sped closer, she could see huge letters on the side—SHINING LIGHT. It was SHINE's polar research ship, an icebreaker that could cut through the polar ice and travel deep into Antarctica. It was also a floating laboratory with SHINE scientists living on board and conducting important environmental research. *Shining Light* was the perfect front for SHINE's

Antarctic surveillance work—agents could monitor activity in the area without drawing attention to themselves and SHINE was helping to protect the environment. It was the SHINE scientists on board *Shining Light* who had detected the disturbing changes in polar temperatures and intercepted the message EJ had decoded.

As *Microlight* came up alongside the icebreaker, like a little fish swimming next to a giant whale, a rope ladder was thrown over the side. A woman's voice boomed out through a loudspeaker on the ship's bridge.

"Welcome *Microlight* and EJ12! We can take things from here. Hold on tight, EJ12, and climb on up."

"Thanks for the ride," EJ told X1, as she grabbed the rope ladder. Agent X1 smiled and spun *Microlight* around—in next to no time, she would be back at SHINE docks and sipping on a hot chocolate.

"Welcome aboard *Shining Light*, EJ12," said the captain, a strong-looking woman with steely blue eyes. "I'm Captain C2C. We'll be able to get you pretty deep into the polar cap on this icebreaker, but once we hit heavy pack ice, we won't be able to go on. Luckily it's early summer here in Antarctica—the ice has been breaking up, allowing us to go farther in. It's a beautiful time of year, but these seas are rough all year round. I hope you have your sea legs, EJ12! Your mission briefing will commence in your cabin in five minutes."

EJ went down to her cabin to prepare for the onboard briefing. It was a small room with only a bed attached to the wall, a porthole looking out to sea and a flat screen on the wall with a small socket to one side. EJ knew what to do. She attached her phone to the socket, keyed in her pin and watched as the screen switched on.

"Welcome aboard, Agent EJ12. Briefing is delayed while new data is being processed. Briefing transmission will commence in ten minutes. You are advised to activate the BEST system in your phone."

While some secret agents worked alone, SHINE believed their agents worked better with backup and so they had developed the BEST agent assistance system.

B.E.S.T. = Brains, Expertise, Support, Tips.

Every agent had a network of people who could help her. The BESTies, as they were known,

were screened by SHINE HQ and cleared to help the agent on missions. Sometimes they helped with tricky codes, sometimes they were useful to get background information and sometimes they were just a friendly voice at the end of the phone when things got tough on a mission. There were two conditions though: the BESTies could ask no questions and an agent could never discuss her work with them when a mission was over. That was okay with the BESTies—who wouldn't want to be part of a top secret mission, even if they couldn't tell anyone about it?

EJ opened the BEST app on her phone, flicked through her contacts and thought hard. A BESTie had to be someone you could trust completely, someone who would never let you down. Elle's profile came up. Elle was reliable. She was always the same, in a good way. Elle didn't change—and neither did her friend Hannah. Both her friends' names were the same backward as they were forward—H-A-N-N-A-H and E-L-L-E—just like her family. No wonder they were so reliable!

Elle had also done a project on Antarctica for geography class last term and she could have useful information. In fact, Elle had useful information about lots of things but particularly the environment. She had just been voted leader of the school Eco Club for that term and was always putting up posters about what people could do to help. Elle was definitely a good choice for a BESTie. But, thought EJ, would Elle still want to help after she had been so hopeless about the party?

Brrrrr-Brrrrr Brrrrr-Brrrrr

It was her phone—and it was Elle! That was weird. "Hi, Elle, I can't talk now," EJ said.

"Oh, right." Elle sounded disappointed, again.

"No, no," said EJ quickly. "I mean, I'm OM." That was spy speak for "on mission," just in case anyone else was listening.

"Oh, right," said Elle, sounding a bit more cheery. "Anyway, I was just calling quickly to say how dumb of me it was to say that you shouldn't go to Nema's party. I'm really sorry."

EJ took a deep breath. "No, it's me that should be sorry and you're right, I don't even like makeup and hairstyles and all that stuff."

Suddenly EJ's phone beeped again.

"Sorry, Elle, but I've got to go," she said. "I've chosen you as my BESTie, I hope that's okay?"

"Of course it is, Em, always. See ya!"

EJ smiled. She was lucky to have such a good friend and she wished she could be a better friend back. She would still have to...

Brrrrr-Brrrrr Brrrrr-Brrrrr

"Stand by, SHINE mission briefing transmission about to commence."

EJ quickly clicked on Elle's profile to upload her as the BESTie, and turned to face the screen. There was A1.

"Welcome aboard *Shining Light*, EJ12. As you know, you are heading toward Antarctica, the world's coldest, windiest and most uninhabited region. Uninhabited by people, that is—the area is simply teeming with animals." And as A1 spoke, images burst on to the screen—whales, fish, birds, leopard seals and, of course, emperor penguins.

"Look closely at this group of penguins, EJ12, because these are the birds that will let you know when you are approaching Emperor Penguin Point. You may come across other penguins, but you need to make sure you find the emperor penguins. Once you see them, you will know that you're close to the target.

"As you know, *Shining Light* will take you as far as it can but, once the pack ice becomes too thick, you will have to travel alone on *Shinemobile 3*. Be careful, EJ, the ice may *look* like a smooth sheet, but that's not always the case. The ice sheets are constantly moving and cracking, creating huge crevasses—make sure you don't fall in one! But if you do, remember your boots. They are there to help.

"You now have just a few hours to get to Emperor Penguin Point and make the payment to Dr. Hill. You will make the payment via your phone," A1 finished.

"But then won't she know it's me?"

"Not with Invisi-Pay, she won't," A1 explained. "All Dr. Hill will see is the deposit and once that hits her account, you should be given an invitation to the party.

"EJ12, you also need to know that since you left SHINE HQ, we have detected unexpected shipping movements in the outlying areas of the region. You may have some company out there—and I don't mean the penguins. For now, the radar shows that *Shining Light* is way ahead, but you must work quickly, EJ12. *SHADOW* will not want any SHINE agents gate-crashing their party."

Gate-crashing—what a modern word for A1! But then again, nothing that woman said or did surprised EJ anymore.

"Oh yes, EJ, I know what you're thinking. Well, this old woman's gate-crashed a few parties in her time too."

How does she do that? thought EJ with a grin.

"I just do!" laughed A1. "Good luck, EJ12. SHINE out."

All that talk about parties and invitations took EJ's thoughts back to school—and Nema. She would just have to tell Nema that she couldn't go to her party. She would do something else with her *real* friends—friends that weren't mean to her or to other people. She could stand up to Nema. Couldn't she?

As EJ thought about Nema again, she began to feel sick to her stomach. But now, unlike this morning before school, it was for real. Then EJ realized that it wasn't just the thought of Nema that was tying her stomach in knots. It was the way the ship was rocking as it knocked against the waves. The waves were getting bigger and bigger, the sea was getting rougher and rougher, and EJ12 was feeling worse and worse. *Oh no, I must be seasick!*

EJ was right. Each time the ship lurched from one side to another, her stomach went with it. For such a

huge boat, it felt like it was being tossed around like a tiny little ball in the ocean. EJ's face started turning green and she wondered how much longer it would be before she and her breakfast parted company.

Just when she thought she had better look for a toilet or a bucket or anything, Captain C2C knocked on her cabin door and entered. She took one look at EJ and laughed, but in a kindly sort of way.

"Still looking for those sea legs I see, EJ12! You better come up on deck, you'll feel better up there. Oh, and you have activated your boat charm, haven't you? That will help too. I have mine on all the time when we're at sea."

EJ looked at Captain C2C's wrist and saw that she had a bracelet similar to hers and a boat charm. Did all agents carry the charms?

"We all carry the charms, EJ, and we all need a little help sometimes," said Captain C2C, smiling. "Activate your boat charm and come up on deck with me."

Gee whizz, lemonfizz! thought EJ. *Am I the only one around here who can't read minds?*

EJ found the little boat charm on her bracelet. It was locked into the wristband so the charm was almost pushing against the inside of her wrist. As she twisted it, the charm began to slowly pulsate. EJ looked up at Captain C2C.

"It works like acupuncture," the captain said. "The charm sends a current through your pulse—that's why it needs to be so close to your wrist. It's an old Chinese method and works a treat with seasickness. It might take a little while, but soon you'll be feeling better. Which is just as well because we're rapidly approaching your drop point."

Out on deck in the fresh air, EJ did indeed feel better. It was, however, the coldest fresh air that EJ had ever experienced—and she had been to some pretty cold places. It was as if the wind was biting her face and she could feel tiny icicles settling on her ears.

"Fresh, isn't it?" chuckled Captain C2C. "We are now in the coldest place on Earth and it's summer—imagine what it's like in winter!"

The ocean swell continued to heave and EJ watched as the black waves rose up and then dropped down again, time after time. At least now she was able to see them coming and that, along with her charm, seemed to be helping with the seasickness.

As she stared out at the black waves, EJ wondered if she might be starting to see things, imagining things that weren't really there. The waves seemed to turn into leaping whales—black-backed whales with white bellies, rising and diving into the swell. *Hold on a minute!* EJ looked harder, her eyes squinting at the water. They really were whales. *Unreal! Well, real, but awesome!*

The whales were dodging the thin ice chunks floating in the sea, rising high up into the air before diving down again, creating enormous splashes as they landed back in the water. There were two whales, a mother and her baby, and it was as if they were having morning play together.

EJ wanted to watch them soar and dive forever, but *Shining Light* continued to push farther and farther south. The floating ice chunks gave way to hard icy sheets that the ship had to break through as it moved forward. The front of the ship rose up and then crashed down again, crushing the ice below. But the farther the ship went, the thicker and harder the ice became, eventually making it impossible to break through.

"This is pretty much as far as we can take you, EJ12. You will need to make your own way across the ice shelf to the island," said Captain C2C. "Proceed to the lower deck and prepare to launch *Shine-mobile 3*."

Shinemobile 3 was part Jet Ski and part snowmobile. It allowed agents to travel on water, land and ice, moving easily from one surface to another. EJ thought it was like riding a motorbike on skis, and probably the most fun you could have outside of the Mission Tube. It was solar-powered, ultralight and moved almost completely without noise.

EJ12 jumped on, turned the key and slowly revved the engine. A large set of doors opened from the lower deck and a ramp was lowered down from the ship. Straight ahead, for as far as the eye could see, there was ice—gleaming bluish ice. EJ locked her phone into a socket and the satellite navigation

screen turned on. EJ keyed in the coordinates of where they thought Emperor Penguin Point was and then slowly eased off the brake, pulled back on the accelerator and slid out onto the ice. She checked the time—EJ needed to get moving—she had less than an hour to make the payment to Dr. Hill.

❄ ❄ ❄

Antarctica was like a desert, a cold, white desert interrupted by giant, jagged icebergs that soared up to the skies. But A1 was right. While the ice might look smooth and flat from a distance, up close it was a much rougher ride. There were deep crevasses everywhere, giant cracks in the ice that could open up without warning. EJ would have to move quickly but carefully.

As she rode along, she saw blobs of gray along the ice. Blobs of gray that were there one moment and gone the next. *Odd*, thought EJ, *and perhaps worth investigating*. She turned toward one blob

and as she got closer she could see that it wasn't a blob at all, it was a seal! A seal that popped its head up onto the ice before diving down again.

"Sorry for thinking you were a blob!" said EJ, laughing. "Let's see what you really are." EJ took a photo of another seal with her phone, pressed "go" and within seconds a photo and text appeared. EJ had used her animal app that could identify every animal in the world.

"You're a Weddell seal," said EJ, "and a very cute one," she added, as she looked at the seal's small head and whiskers and a mouth that almost looked like it was smiling. The animal app told her that Weddell seals spend nearly all their time under the water, popping up through cracks or holes in the ice. The seal seemed to look at EJ and then dived down again, back on its way—which is what EJ needed to be doing too.

She pulled away from the seal hole and sped up a bit. Way up above in the crystal clear blue sky, a solitary bird was circling overhead. She took another photo with her phone. The bird was a skua, like a seagull but browner and bigger. And meaner. EJ saw it and wondered what it was hunting.

A bit farther on, she saw penguins, hundreds, maybe even thousands of them coming out of the ocean and starting to waddle across the ice. Emperor penguins? She wasn't sure. They didn't seem big enough. Again she took a photo, pressed "go" and waited. The information appeared on the screen, confirming EJ's thoughts. These ones were Adélie penguins and they were indeed smaller than the emperor penguins. But it wasn't all bad news. The Adélie penguin ground was not far off from where the emperor penguins should be—and where EJ12 needed to be. She was close, but she needed to hurry.

EJ switched the Shinemobile to turbo and sped across the ice shelf and it was not too long before another black mass loomed up in the distance—more penguins. And, as she got closer, EJ could see that these ones were taller and with distinctive bright-yellow ear patches. There was no need for EJ to check her animal app. She had found the emperor penguins, which was just as well because she needed to make the payment in ten minutes.

EJ kept her cool and remembered that A1 had said that there was an abandoned hut near the penguin grounds. These huts had been used by the early explorers but were now deserted, or were they? SHINE thought Dr. Hill might now be using one. EJ scanned the area with her binoculars but could see nothing. She rechecked her map. According to the map, there should be a hut on the other side of the mountain just ahead. EJ sped on around the base of the mountain and soon found herself outside an old wooden hut, built right up against the mountain where it would have been protected from blizzards. It looked as if it had been there for years. Maybe too many years—with loose planks and tin falling off the roof, the hut had obviously seen better days. A metal sign was hanging from one corner of the roof.

Wow, 1950, that's old! thought EJ. *EPP—Emperor Penguin Point—this is it.*

There was no way she could take *Shinemobile 3* inside with her, so she hit the green button marked "ED" next to the ignition and waited. Eco-Deco was just one of the clever eco-friendly **SHINE** inventions that ensured their agents didn't leave their gadgets lying around all over the world. (Not only might they be discovered, but it would be littering!) EJ watched as *Shinemobile 3* began to decompose. It was a smelly process, like burping—or sometimes, worse, farting—and EJ knew better than to stand too close. She moved back and as she waited, she again noticed the large skua circling above her. Odd. She then heard a large belch from the Shinemobile and turned back to see that it had not decomposed completely but transformed. There was now a purple snowboard lying on the ice. *Cool*, thought EJ, as she picked it up and slung it over her shoulder. *That may be useful later...*

EJ moved closer to the hut and as she did, she noticed something odd. Attached to the very old, broken-down hut was a very modern, not-broken-down steel door. And on the door was a keypad and small sign.

HNVITED DUESTS MNLY.

DWIPE XARD IND QAIT.

What language is that? Not one that EJ recognized (and, having completed the SHINE intensive language course, she could, besides other things, ask for a hot chocolate in fifteen different languages). So if it wasn't a language, EJ decided that it must be a code.

But what sort of code? EJ looked and looked, but nothing jumped out at her. She wrinkled her nose and kept looking, waiting for a pattern to appear. *You never really know what you are looking at with codes,* thought EJ. *Does one letter stand for another, does a number really mean a letter, is something missing or is something added? Hmmm...* She had no idea, but she had to hurry—there were just five minutes left to make the payment.

EJ looked at the first word:

HNVITED

The word sort of looked normal, except for the H. It was the same with the second word:

DUESTS

In fact, it was only the first letter of each word that looked out of place. EJ wondered what would happen if she took all the first letters out. She used her finger to draw a line through the first letter of each word on the frosty surface of the sign.

HNVITED DUESTS MNLY.
DWIPE XARD AND QAIT.

Hmmm, not as helpful as I thought, said EJ to herself. *It still looks weird but maybe slightly less weird than before. I wonder what would happen if I put different letters back. Worth a try, but which ones?* EJ studied the words for a while and then suddenly she saw it.

I G O
HNVITED DUESTS MNLY.
S C A W
DWIPE XARD AND QAIT.

Invited guests? Guests, party guests—I must be in the right place. EJ then looked at the keypad next to the sign. It was just like a mini automatic teller machine at the bank. *Swipe card.* A1's guess had been right. Emperor Penguin Point was where EJ had to make the payment. But had she gotten there first? There was only one way to find out.

Quickly and with only seconds to spare, EJ took out her Invisi-Pay card and swiped. She confirmed the pin and pressed "OK" for the payment to proceed.

The screen flashed and the words "Confirm amount" appeared.

EJ keyed in "$20,000,000," taking a deep breath at the thought of such a huge sum of money, and for a moment she was distracted by wondering how much chocolate that would buy. Then she pressed "OK" and almost immediately, a silver envelope emerged from a slot under the keypad. *The invitation? It certainly looks like one and, for that amount of money, it better be* some *party*.

EJ ripped open the envelope and pulled out a silver card with black writing. A small silver whistle fell out and landed on the ice. As she picked it up, her hand brushed the ice and for a moment, her skin felt warm. *Strange*, she thought, but forgot about it as she slipped the whistle into her pocket and began to read the card inside.

> *Congratulations!*
>
> *Your payment has been accepted and you are now a partner in Dr. Caterina Hill's Volpol Pipeline Water Company. Together we will be rich. Open the door, come inside and see a sneak preview of my genius. Then just whistle and you will be whisked away to the greatest party of all–mine, of course! Party starts at 6pm sharp.*
>
> *Brilliantly yours,*
>
> *Dr. C. Hill*

Volpol. *That* was the first word of the code, but what could it mean?

EJ turned the handle of the door, pushed it open and gasped. It certainly wasn't what she expected

from the outside. Inside, there were no more old pieces of wood, there was only stainless steel—stainless steel walls, a stainless steel table and then another door, a stainless steel door with the words DANGER VOLPOL PIPE ACCESS POINT on it.

On the table was a bottle of water. EJ picked up the bottle and read the label:

Water. This was about water? But how? There was nothing else in the room to give her any clues so EJ walked over to the second door and tried to open it, but it was locked. She took her charm key, twisted it and inserted it into the lock. With only a little jiggle, the key turned and the door opened.

If EJ was surprised by the first room, she was completely stunned by where she was now. She stepped onto a metal platform overlooking a huge hole that ran both deep down into the ground and straight upward. Lit by small lights fixed along the rock wall, the tunnel ran up and down the center of the mountain and in the middle of the tunnel ran a large pipe. The Volpol Pipe.

EJ leaned over to touch the pipe but quickly jumped back—it was hot! *Hot? How is that possible? Here in Antarctica?* And then EJ realized that the pipe wasn't the only thing that was hot. As she stood there, she felt her feet warming up through her boots. The metal of the platform was hot—hotter than the sidewalk on a summer's day. All the ice on her boots had melted and she was now standing in a pool of water—a pool of *hot* water.

Where is the heat coming from? EJ had no idea, but she knew someone who might—Elle. Elle had called her geography project "Amazing Antarctica —Unbelievable Facts." She had spent ages on it, uncovering little known facts and figures about the area. She might know why it was hot when it should be cold. It was certainly worth a try. It was time to use the BEST app. EJ phoned her friend, who answered immediately.

"Hi again, what's up?" Elle knew from the special ring tone that it was EJ calling—EJ OM and in need of Elle's help.

"Hi, Elle. You know your project on Antarctica?" said EJ. "I don't suppose you found out any amazing facts about hot things as well as cold?"

Elle chuckled. "You mean you weren't listening?"

"Um, I think I had a guitar lesson during some of your presentation," said EJ quickly. "But please, Elle, it's important!"

"Well yes, you wouldn't believe it, but there are at least three volcanoes at the South Pole and they are all still active. Can you believe that? One of nature's hottest things in the middle of nature's coldest environment. In fact, *that* was the number one amazing fact in my project. Why do you ask?"

"Because I think I might be standing in one of those volcanoes."

"That's awesome," Elle replied. "Did you know that the lava level is deep down in the Earth?" Elle loved sharing her facts. "Its intense heat can cause glacier ice to melt leading to increases in meltwater."

"Meltwater, what's that?" asked EJ, remembering the water bottle label.

"It's just what you would think it is, Em. Water melted from the ice. Some people think we could use the volcanic heat to create more meltwater to make more drinking water, but that would be a disaster. Sea levels would rise and global warming would be even more out of control than it already is. Luckily though, no one has been able to work out how to do it."

"I think maybe someone now has," said EJ, looking at the pipeline. Shivers ran down her spine as she realized what Caterina Hill was up to. *She's using the volcanic heat to melt ice to make drinking water bottled as "Chill." But how does she collect the water? How does the Volpol Pipe work and can I stop it?* EJ needed to find out, quickly.

"Elle, I've got to go."

"OK, but Em, if you are thinking what I think you are thinking, you can't let that someone get away with this."

"I won't."

EJ wasn't going to let her friend down, again. She was going to stop Caterina, even if she wasn't exactly sure how.

EJ stood still, thinking about her next move. She needed to make another phone call, this time to SHINE HQ. She had hardly pushed the speed dial number on her phone when it was picked up at the other end.

"Hello, EJ12," said A1. "What's happening out there?"

"I think I'm getting warmer," EJ replied. "I cracked another code, the payment has been made, and I'm pretty sure we now know the *what* as well as the *where* and the *who,* but I am still a bit unsure about the *how*. I think Dr. Hill is using volcanic heat energy to melt the polar ice cap. Oh, and I now know the first word of the first code. It's VOLPOL."

"What *is* Volpol?" asked A1.

"It's an enormous pipe coming out from deep down in what I think is a volcano. I can hear gushing coming from inside the pipe. Do you think maybe the volcanic heat is making water in the pipe hot? That would mean the heat could be taken somewhere else."

"That's possible. Hold on," said A1. "Let me check some things on volcanic heat." EJ could hear the sound of A1 on the keyboard and then, "You're right, EJ. Water in the pipe could be being heated as it passes close to the hot rock around the volcano. But why transport the heat?"

"I'm pretty sure Caterina is melting ice for bottled water. She's turning the polar cap into a Polar Tap."

"Good work, EJ. With drought in many countries, the price of water is skyrocketing. Water is the new gold and Caterina loves gold. I wouldn't be surprised if she was prepared to melt the whole polar ice cap for money—a chilling thought indeed. What else do you know about the pipeline?"

"Not much more. I need to follow it."

"You do that, EJ, and find out how to shut it down before it is too late. But don't be late for the party either. We need to catch Caterina. Put your best boot forward, EJ12. SHINE out."

Best boot forward? What does that mean? As EJ looked up the tunnel, she wondered how she was going to climb up the tunnel with nothing to hold on to except a boiling hot pipe. She looked down at her feet and then smiled. Why didn't she think of that before? Her special issue SHINE boots.

Chapter 11

EJ clicked her boots together. The boots became flippers. *No, that won't help,* she thought, as she clicked again to get rid of the flippers and then clicked once again. This time she felt her boots rise up, and out came suction soles, with the words "For use on hot and cold surfaces" printed on the side. These suction soles were made from an unmeltable, unfreezable micro-rubber. They would stick to anything—including mountain walls and hot pipelines—yet release as you lifted your feet.

Keeping one foot on the platform, EJ stretched out her leg and put the other boot onto the pipe. It gripped fast, but as she lifted her leg, it came away easily. Perfect, but how would she pull herself up? She needed something to grip the rock wall with as she climbed—a pick ideally, just like the one on her charm bracelet but obviously slightly bigger. She twisted the little charm, there was a loud pop and the mini pick became a maxi pick. Lucky charms indeed!

EJ plunged the pick into the wall and began to climb. She would swing the pick up into the rock, make sure it held and then bring her feet up along the pipe. It was hard work, but with the super grip of the suction soles she was able to move up the tunnel wall quickly, following the pipeline higher and higher. *Thank goodness for the lights,* EJ thought, *I wouldn't want to be in this tunnel in the dark.*

For most of the climb, the tunnel had been rock, but now it had changed to ice. *I must be at the top of the mountain now and this is the ice layer,* thought EJ. *I should soon be at the surface.*

Then suddenly the direction of the pipeline changed. EJ had expected that it would finally push out through the top of the ice, but instead it turned and ran along under the ice layer horizontally. EJ was practically walking upside down as she began to follow the pipe in this new direction.

She also noticed that the pipe had now split in two. There was still the red-hot pipe and this was so close to the surface that the heat from it was melting the ice above, but now, just below it, there was another, larger pipe. This pipe was different though. It was a half-pipe sitting under the hot pipe, as if it was waiting to catch something from above. And it was. It was catching water, the large drips of water that the hot pipe was melting. Meltwater, water that then flowed down the pipeline. But to where?

EJ was never going to find out in time walking one slow suction-step at a time. She would need to get up to the surface and follow the pipeline from above. She looked up at the thick ice. Using her pick would take forever. She would need something else, and watching the water drip down into the catchment pipe gave EJ an idea. She took out her phone and activated the laser app and pointed the red-hot beam toward the ice. Within minutes she had scorched an EJ-sized hole through the ice to the surface. Swinging the pick up, she pulled herself out of the hole and onto the icy peak of the mountain. She clicked her suction soles back into her boots and stood up and looked around.

EJ could just see the little hut way down below and she could also make out the path of the pipeline running under the ice. It ran down the mountain and then along the ice plain with the melting ice forming a huge crack through the ice. If you hadn't known the pipeline was there, you would have just assumed that the ice was naturally melting and shifting, creating natural crevasses. You couldn't actually see the pipe. So the scientists could see that the ice was melting but not why. *Caterina is clever,* thought EJ, *evil but clever.*

And then there were the penguins, thousands of Emperor penguins. In fact there was nearly more penguin black than there was ice white. It was like a sea of black—a noisy, squawking, waddling sea of penguins.

And there, still circling above it all, was that skua again. What could it be looking at? EJ took out her binoculars and scanned the penguin colony. Between the legs of the larger penguins sat fluffy, gray chicks. Maybe the skua was hungry and was looking for unprotected chicks? EJ remembered her briefing—at this time of year the penguin chicks would have hatched and would be waiting with their fathers for the mothers to return from sea with food. While already quite large, the chicks still relied on their parents for food. It was the mothers that EJ had passed on her way to Emperor Penguin Point. *Come to think of it, why aren't the mothers already back with their families?* Then EJ saw why.

The crevasse the pipeline path had created had cut straight through the middle of the penguins' breeding ground. It was going to prevent many of the mother penguins returning to the breeding ground and reuniting with their families. EJ scanned the breeding ground again. The pipeline had created such a long and deep crevasse that access to the sea was completely cut off, except for little breakaway blocks of ice, like mini-icebergs, floating in pools of melted water. And sitting on one of those blocks was a penguin chick, stranded. And above it, that skua was still there, circling. Then it began to swoop, lower and lower toward the chick.

"Don't you even think about it!" yelled E J, stamping her foot. She was standing on the edge and as her boots hit the ice, she heard a cracking noise and felt the ice give way beneath her. Suddenly she was falling fast.

As she fell, she felt something hard against her back—her snowboard! E J reached back, grabbed her board, pulled it down and clicked her boots together. *Please let there be jet-pack heels,* she thought to herself. *Please!* She clicked again and the suction soles popped out. Another click—stilts. *Aaaaaaaaaargh!* SHINE really needed a better system than this. Still falling, she clicked again and finally a jet pack emerged from each heel.

EJ checked that her boots were locked to the snowboard and pulled the laces to activate her boots.

Varoom!

The jet packs kicked in and EJ was now flying down the steep cliff on her snowboard. She could steer her way down the cliff with her body, and then onto the ice plain below, jumping over rocks and crevasses, and all the time trying to follow the path of the pipeline and keeping her eye on the baby penguin and the skua. EJ saw the big crevasse approaching and the chick stranded on its floating ice block nearby. She needed to think fast. Pulling her laces hard, she kicked up a gear to turbo charge. She would have to pull this off with pinpoint accuracy.

Just as the skua started to sweep down, EJ soared up and knocked the skua out of the way. Then bouncing down on the ice block, she scooped up the chick. Holding the bird tightly between her legs, she soared up again before landing back on the ice shelf. The skua dived again, but it was too late, the chick was now hidden inside EJ's jacket.

EJ suddenly realized just how smelly one chick could be. "You must really like your fish," she told the chick, wishing she had a nose clip charm as well.

EJ pulled her laces again, moving down a gear and into cruise control, following the pipeline. Hovering on top of it, EJ could now see the water pouring into the lower pipeline and it was steaming, still hot from the melting process. Something else would have to happen to it before it was ready for bottling. She would have to keep following the pipeline to find out. As she boarded along she looked up and there again was the skua, high up in the sky never very far behind, following her.

Chapter 12

Scanning with her binoculars as she boarded along, EJ finally saw the end of the pipeline. It disappeared into something that looked a bit like a factory building. EJ switched off her jet-boots and jumped off her board—she would need to move quietly in case anyone was around.

With the jet-boots quiet she could now hear some rather impatient squawking coming from inside her jacket. Someone was hungry, but what did little penguins eat? Then EJ remembered her bracelet again and the little penguin charm. EJ twisted the charm and it extended to reveal a tiny bottle labeled "Concentrated Penguin Nutrients, Contains Traces of Fish" and an eyedropper. *How does SHINE always know these things?*

EJ held the chick's beak open and squeezed in a few drops. Its big eyes blinked in a slightly surprised way, but then it opened its mouth for more—clearly a successful recipe! *Okay, that's enough for now, my fluffy little friend.* EJ carefully put the chick back inside her jacket. *Now stay there—and stay warm. I've got some work to do.*

EJ pressed the Eco-Deco button on the snowboard, which luckily dissolved with just a few quick, reasonably quiet farts. She clicked on her boots to retract the jet packs and clicked her heels again to search for the ice skates. And then her phone went. It was SHINE HQ.

"EJ," said A1. "You really need to hurry. We have just received a temperature status report from *Shining Light* and the news is not good. Both the temperature and the water levels are now dangerously high. We must shut this thing down before it causes any more damage. By our scientists' calculations, you have one hour before the temperature reaches an unstoppable meltdown level. Your alarm has been set on your phone, EJ. You must hurry. We're counting on you—the whole world is!"

Well, just as long as there's no pressure then, thought EJ. *I don't work so well under pressure.* She fastened her skates and glided off toward the building ahead. As she got closer, she could see that the pipeline fed directly into one side of the building. Two smaller pipes, one red, one blue, came out the other side.

EJ walked around the side of the building and found a door with the words SWITCH ROOM on it. EJ pushed on the door, but it was locked. Again she took out her trusty key charm, twisted it and pushed it into the lock, jiggled it around and the lock turned. *I'm in!*

But she wasn't exactly sure *what* she was in. The incoming pipe fed into a large metal tank. On the front of it there was some kind of control box

with buttons and levers, flashing lights, dials and switches and beeping noises. Two pipes came out of the other side of the tank. One was red and it fed back into the pipeline and the other was blue and it shot out the other side of the tank. Right in the middle of the control box, there were two levers with screens above them. The first screen flashed words in blue and the second screen flashed words in red. But not really words. *Code. More code. Gee whizz, lemonfizz!* thought EJ, *doesn't anyone just use normal words anymore?*

DLOC OT TOH
LETOH DNA SKNAT OT

TOH OT DLOC
TNIOP NIUGNEP ROREPME OT

And now the alarm app on EJ's phone was flashing too. *Only thirty minutes to meltdown!* Time was running out, but the letters on the screens meant nothing to EJ. No matter which way she looked at them, the words remained nonsense.

Don't panic, she thought. *Keep a cool head.* She looked around for clues. To the side of each pipe was a tap. She turned the tap on the blue pipe and water gushed out—cool water. She tried the tap on the red pipe—hot steam gushed out. And then EJ got it. This machine was like a giant water cooler and heater in one. It cooled down the polar meltwater so that it could be used as drinking water and it kept volcanic heat moving through the pipeline across the ice shelf. Then it clicked in EJ's mind: Volpol. Volcanic and Polar. Hot and Cold.

EJ studied the screens again and now that she had figured out the purpose of the machine, the meaning of the words leapt out at her. They were all back to front, just like what Dr. Hill was doing with the ice.

Or were they? Was she right? What if she was wrong? EJ panicked for just a split second. Then she looked at the screen one more time. She felt suddenly very calm. Yes. She was sure she was right.

HOT TO COLD
TO TANKS AND HOTEL

COLD TO HOT
TO EMPEROR PENGUIN POINT

Back to front! thought EJ. *If I pull the levers the other way could I reverse the process? Could I send the cold water gushing back down the pipeline to refreeze the ice? Could it be that simple?* With only minutes to spare, EJ decided it had to be. She pulled the lever leading to the red pipe down. There was a loud whirring noise and then a clank and a gush. And then EJ noticed the red pipe was slowly changing color, moving from red to orange to yellow and blue. It was working; EJ had reversed the melting process.

She pulled the other lever. Again, she heard the loud whirring noise followed by a clank and a gush, and slowly the blue pipe turned red, sending warm water off toward the tanks and the hotel.

The hotel, the ice hotel! EJ had completely forgotten about Dr. Hill's party. She may have just stopped the polar ice cap from melting and quite probably prevented an environmental disaster, but she didn't feel like celebrating. She knew she would still have to stand up to Dr. Caterina Hill and she felt all her courage melt away at the very thought.

As she turned to leave the Switch Room, EJ spied what looked like a fire extinguisher on the wall. It was a sort of cylinder with a pump hose attached. She looked more closely and read the label, "Volpol Portachill." She pulled the nozzle and sprayed. The pressure release almost knocked her over, but it was what came out that surprised her most—it was ice. The spray froze whatever it hit, in this case EJ's foot. It was frozen rock solid. She could barely lift it and could only just walk. She was certainly dressed to chill now!

EJ packed the Portachill in her backpack. *That might come in handy if I find myself in hot water*, she thought, and laughed at her own joke. Then she clicked her heels and, even with one boot iced, her

skates reappeared. She turned toward the blue pipe that had now turned fire-engine red. *This should lead me all the way to the ice hotel…it's party time!*

Chapter 13

The ice hotel was like nothing EJ had ever seen before. If you could imagine a large city hotel with fountains and statues and lights, all completely made out of ice, then that was what EJ was looking at. The problem was that EJ couldn't figure out how to get in—all the doors were iced shut.

But EJ didn't really mind—she already had cold feet about having to face Dr. Hill, and it wasn't just because she had iced one of them with the Portachill. She had a nagging feeling that she wasn't going to be able to handle Dr. Hill—the same kind

of hopeless feeling she had when she was trying to deal with Nema back at school. Perhaps she could just forget this part of the mission—that would be a lot easier. *After all, I've foiled the doctor's evil plan, so do I really need to go to the party? Maybe I'll just cool my heels out here for a while,* EJ thought, as she leaned against an ice pillar.

EJ's phone beeped. It was a text message from Elle.

GOOD LUCK EM, U CAN DO THIS. I KNOW U CAN. BFF ELLE

EJ smiled. Best Friends Forever. Elle knew how to make her feel good. She was a BESTie whether she was called or not. And Elle was right—she could do this. She would stand up to Caterina, if only she could find a way in. Then, as EJ walked forward a little, she felt the ground under her feet give way and once again, she was falling...

...and then landing again. EJ found herself on a lovely soft black rug in the middle of a silvery-white room—a beautiful room in a hard, cold way. The shiny ice-blue walls were draped with ice curtains and ice tables were dotted around, holding ice vases with long, pointy ice flowers. It all looked very fancy, but it was not the kind of room you could just flop down and watch some movies in—which was much more EJ's style. In the middle, there was a large, white, egg-like swivel chair, with its back to EJ. And from inside the chair came a voice—a cold, hard, slightly croaky voice that sounded as if its owner needed to cough.

"Thanks for dropping in, EJ12. I've been expecting you."

The chair spun around and EJ came face-to-face with Dr. Caterina Hill.

For one really horrible moment, EJ thought she was looking at Nema—or at least an older version of her. But even Nema would have been much less scary than this seriously weird woman. Dr. Caterina Hill was wearing black skinny-leg snow pants topped with a padded gold ski jacket, the hood edged with silver-gray fur. On one finger she had a huge diamond —or was it ice?—ring and her nails were long and painted silver, almost like claws. Perched on a stand next to Caterina was a skua, its eyes as black, as piercing and as mean as its mistress's. Both sets of eyes were now staring straight at EJ.

"I am so glad you're here, EJ12, although I must say you took your time. I thought you might be late for my little party."

"I don't see any party," said EJ coolly.

"Oh, you know what they say, two's a party and three's a crowd," Dr. Hill smirked. "And after all, it's a party especially for you. Did you really think I didn't know you were coming? You walked right into my trap."

EJ looked confused.

"Don't you worry your unpretty head about it. I have eyes everywhere," said Dr. Hill, stroking the skua. And it was then that EJ recognized the bird—it was the same one that had been following her since she left *Shining Light*. Now she noticed that it had a small camera tied to its leg. Caterina had seen everything that had happened to her.

"***SHADOW*** will pay me double for my water and one of **SHINE**'s top agents," Dr. Hill continued.

"Except that you don't have any water anymore," said EJ quietly—so quietly that it was almost impossible to hear her.

"What? Speak up? Cat got your tongue? Or should that be 'Caterina got your tongue?'" Dr. Hill cackled cruelly.

EJ took a deep breath. She was suddenly really tired of mean people saying mean things. "I said, 'You don't have any water anymore.'"

"Don't be ridiculous," Dr. Hill scoffed. "My pipeline is pumping millions of gallons of pure melted ice water into my tanks as we speak. And soon those tanks will be rolling their way onto ***SHADOW*** tankers.

SHADOW will control the world's water market and I will be rolling in millions of dollars!"

"So you're doing all this just for money? What about the South Pole? What about the emperor penguins?" EJ pleaded.

"Bah! Penguin, shmenguin. I couldn't care less. All those smelly penguin chicks can fall in the sea and drown for all I care. Ha-ha-ha!"

"You're not going to get away with this, Dr. Hill!" said EJ defiantly.

"Oh really, EJ 'zero,' and who is going to stop me? Certainly not SHINE—those silly do-gooders back at SHINE HQ couldn't stop me if they tried. That silly A1 with her silly mottoes—she had her chance but chose not to pay. And now she really will pay."

"No she won't. I'm here and I'll stop you!"

"Don't make me laugh, EJ 'zero,' you couldn't stop anything."

That did it for EJ12. She looked straight at Dr. Hill and instead of seeing someone scary, she just saw someone with bad nails and a cold heart—someone she could stand up to. She was not going to back down or melt away this time!

"I already have, Dr. Hill. I think you'll find that your pipes have been switched. Cold water is now heading back to refreeze the polar ice cap and hot water is on its way here. In fact, now that I think about it, your ice flowers are looking a little droopy..."

Caterina sat up with a start. Sure enough, the hot water now being pumped around the ice hotel was slowly melting the ice tables, the ice vases and the pointy ice flowers inside them.

"How did you do that?" Dr. Hill turned back to EJ with a frosty glare. "Well, no matter, I will simply switch them back again—after I have dealt with you, EJ12."

"Maybe you should just chill out for a while, Caterina..."

"How dare you, you little nobody. I'll..."

But that was far as Dr. Hill got. EJ pulled the Portachill from her backpack and sprayed it full blast toward the ice queen. Almost instantly, Dr. Caterina Hill was snap-chilled into an ice statue. She was finally as cold as she looked.

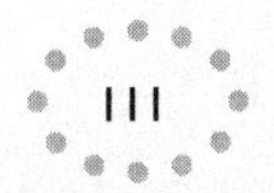

EJ heaved a big sigh of relief. She gave Caterina another quick spray with the Portachill. With a few more blasts, she would remain snap-chilled for quite some time and she would be fine once she thawed out—in prison.

While Caterina was now frozen, her ice hotel was slowly melting around her. *Hot and cold, cold and hot, everything seems to be one thing or the other at the moment,* thought EJ. *It would be nice to be somewhere in the middle for a while.* Then a little squeaking and rustling sound in the lining of her jacket broke into her thoughts—she had nearly forgotten about the little penguin chick!

Gently she lifted it out. "Time for some more food, is it?" The little chick looked up with its mouth wide-open, waiting. "I'll take that as a yes," laughed EJ, as she took out the charm bottle and dropped some more food into the little penguin's beak. "But now we need to get you back to your family and make sure your mom has been able to get back to the breeding ground."

As she was putting the penguin chick back into her jacket, something fell out of her backpack and onto the ground. It was the little silver whistle that came with Caterina's "party" invitation. She had forgotten all about it but was curious as to what it did. She picked up the whistle and blew. It made a long high-pitched sound.

Piiiiiip!

EJ blew it again. She had no idea what it could have been for.

Then EJ heard a noise approaching from a distance. The noise got louder as it got closer. *Dogs barking? Here?* EJ turned to see a sled racing toward the melting ice hotel. It was pulled by six excited husky dogs, barking madly and wagging their tails. A sign on the side of the sled said "Ice Hotel Express."

"Well," said EJ to no one in particular. "Dr. Hill can't be all bad if she likes dogs, but who's going to look after them now?" And then she heard a different kind of bark—a little yap—and to her delight, a little snow-white puppy jumped off the sled and half scampered and half tumbled up to EJ.

"Aren't you beautiful!" exclaimed EJ, holding out her arms. The little pup jumped all over her, rewarding her with wet puppy licks. *Yucky, but kind of nice too.*

"Okay, let's get going then," EJ told the dogs. She climbed onto the sled with the puppy next to her, gave the reins a slight pull and the huskies began a slow trot. Using the reins to steer, EJ turned the sled back along the path of the pipeline crevasse,

which was now slowly but surely disappearing as the ice refroze.

The dogs were strong and fast and together they sprinted across the ice as one. They seemed to know exactly where to go, how to avoid crevasses and bumps, and where to find the smoothest, fastest path. They ran up a ridge and as they came over the top, EJ could see that her pipe plan had worked. The crevasse that had split the nesting ground in two had covered over and there were penguins everywhere. As she zoomed in with her binoculars, she could see that the birds were all waddling around in threes—two adult birds and a chick in each group. The penguin families were back together again and, by the look of those chubby and not so little chicks, they were all well fed.

She guided the sled down the hill and onto the plain but was careful to keep her distance from the penguins. As the dogs paced along, EJ continued to scan the breeding ground, and then she found what she was looking for—two adult penguins, waddling around as if they too were searching for something.

EJ guided the sled as close as she dared and then stopped. She took the little penguin chick out of her jacket and placed it gently on the ice. It began to squeak and squawk loudly and the two older penguins quickly waddled toward it.

"Slowly now," whispered EJ to the huskies. "We don't want to spoil a family reunion!" And as the sled slid away, EJ looked back to see the little chick climbing onto the larger penguin's feet, its mouth wide-open. Its mother was more than happy to oblige with food.

Mission accomplished! thought EJ with a smile. *All of them!* It was time for SHINE Home Delivery. EJ turned to look at the huskies. *I hope there's enough room for all of us.* She took out her phone and pressed 4-6-6-3 on the keypad. A woman's voice answered immediately.

"SHINE Home Delivery Service—straight to your door, anytime, anywhere."

"Agent EJ12 here, requesting home delivery for ...um...eight!"

SHINE Home Delivery Service was used to

EJ picking up extra passengers on her missions, but eight was a new record.

"Well, only one human," EJ explained. "The rest are dogs—and one of them is very small," she added, hoping that might help.

The woman at the other end laughed. "No problem, EJ12. We have your coordinates. A chopper will be dispatched from *Shining Light*. It will be a tight squeeze, but you should all fit. Stay on the line, EJ12. I need to connect you to HQ."

There was a beep and then a familiar voice.

"Well done, EJ12. Another successful mission," said A1.

"Polar ice cap temperatures restored to normal, emperor penguin colony reunited, ice-water factory shut down, ice hotel melted and Dr. Caterina Hill is . . . er. . .out of action," reported EJ.

"Out of action?" pondered A1.

"Let's just say she's pretty chilled," said EJ, smiling to herself. "And she won't be going anywhere in a hurry."

"Our cleanup team will take care of her and the

rest of her factory," said A1. "Soon no one will ever know that she—or you—were there. Good job, EJ. That was a tough mission, but you did it, just as we knew you would. And it wouldn't be an EJ12 mission without a few extra passengers to pick up, I hear. We can take the older dogs—we have a training camp in the mountains that they will love. But the puppy will need a home immediately. Do you think you could look after it, at least for a while, until she is ready to start training?"

"You bet!" yelled EJ12, completely overlooking the small fact that she hadn't asked her mom if she could have a dog yet.

"I think we will call you Pip," she said, as she scratched behind the little pup's ears. "P-I-P, just like the whistle sound that brought you to me. What do you think, Pip?" EJ took the sloppy lick on her face as a yes.

"Okay then," said A1, laughing. "That's sorted. And I hope you had everything you needed for your mission."

"Absolutely A1, although I think there was one charm I didn't use." EJ shook her bracelet and reached for the little silver heart charm. She twisted it and an inscription appeared: "Brave voices melt cold deeds." Perhaps she had used it after all.

Chapter 15

When Emma woke up the next morning she was still feeling a little sleepy. It was another school morning, but at least this one started with a very cute and fluffy puppy licking her face.

There were two good things about the puppy. The first thing was obvious—Emma finally had one, and Pip was the cutest puppy she could have dreamed of. The second thing was her mom. Emma remembered the discussion the night before when she returned home.

"What's that under your arm, Em?"

"Um, a puppy."

"A real puppy? A hair-shedding puppy? A peeing-on-the-floor puppy? A puppy we haven't talked about getting?" asked Mom sternly.

"Um, yes, all of those things."

"Well I'm sorry, Em, but it will just have to go back where it came from."

"Er...I really don't think it can," Emma started nervously.

"Can you please give me one good reason why not?"

Emma couldn't. She wasn't allowed to reveal that she was a SHINE agent, not even to her mom. And seeing as she couldn't even convince her mom she was sick yesterday, how was she going to explain this one?

And then suddenly Mom smiled, looked around as if to check that no one else was listening and whispered, "I think I understand, Em. Come with me for a minute."

Not another talk! Emma groaned, and then wondered why they were opening Mom's closet.

"Emma, I'm going to show you something."

Mom pressed a button inside the closet door and a panel at the back slid aside to reveal a small room —a small secret room with a laptop and photos on the wall. There were photos of Mom up trees, on mountains, underwater and with baby animals—lion cubs, tiny snakes, koalas and more. And there were certificates, lots of certificates, all of them with a small familiar logo in the corner—the SHINE logo.

"You're part of SHINE too," Emma gasped.

"Well, I used to be. Agent SJ retired some time ago." Mom winked. "So I know about the baby animal thing and I think I understand what might have happened. But Emma, this is our secret. A1 gave me clearance to tell you because she thought I might be useful for your BEST network. No one else must ever know, not even the boys."

"Mom, that's so cool," said Emma, giving her mom a hug. *A secret between the girls of the family!*

"But Em," said Mom seriously, "no more pets—not even cute ones like your puppy friend here! And now, off to bed or you will be too tired for school."

School...Nema. Emma had forgotten all about her.

Emma knew she would have to talk to Nema this time. Rather than getting all hot under the collar, she felt calm, cool even. She jumped out of the car, waved her mom good-bye and almost skipped into school. Then, as she approached the classroom, she heard a familiar voice talking loudly, and meanly, to another girl.

"As if, Alisha. Of course you can't play with us, you don't know the dance moves!"

It was Nema. *Who else?*

"Hi, Emma, where did you disappear to yesterday? We were making plans for the party. At least, the girls who are coming were," said Nema, with a sideways glance at Alisha.

Emma took a deep breath. "Hi, Alisha, what a great hair band! Hi, Nema, I had a really bad cold, but I'm fine now. But Nema," said Emma, taking a big breath before saying in a loud voice, "I don't think I'll be able to come to your party."

Just then the school bus pulled up at the gate and a group of girls, including Elle and Hannah, skipped down the stairs, laughing and chatting happily. Elle raced up to her friend and gave her a big hug.

"Hey, Em, feeling any warmer? What's happening?"

"Nothing for you to worry about, Elle," snapped Nema and then she turned back to Emma. "What do you mean you're not coming? That's ridiculous, it's going to be the best party of the year." Nema fixed Emma with an icy stare—but this time it wasn't going to work. Emma didn't have the Portachill anymore, but now she knew how to deal with mean people like Nema.

"No, I'm not coming, Nema, but not because I've got a cold. I'm not coming because I think you have been horrible to Elle and I don't want to be your friend if that's how you treat people." Emma turned to look at Elle, who was smiling back at her.

"Well," said Nema, sounding a bit shaky, slightly flustered even. "Who cares? Actually..." and her voice started to sound stronger and harder again, "I

was only asking you because my mom said I had to."
Then Nema turned to Hannah with a sickly sweet smile. "Han, why don't you come instead—you were on my B-list."

Everyone gasped. *B-list?*

"No thanks, Nema," said Hannah calmly. "I've got other plans." And the three girls turned and walked away with big smiles on their faces.

"Thanks, Em," said Elle. "You were great the way you stood up to her."

"We all were," said Emma. "And now let's plan our own party!"

❄ ❄ ❄

The next Saturday, Elle and Hannah came over to Emma's house for a sleepover. They had decided to have their own movie party, but it was slightly less stylish than Nema's—pajamas instead of dresses, Ugg boots instead of party shoes and crazy hair styles instead of makeovers. It was cozy rather than cool, which was actually much cooler. The three girls lay on the floor with beanbags, quilts and pillows. Pip was nestled in among them and they were stocked up with plenty of popcorn, marshmallows and hot chocolate.

"So, which movie?" asked Emma.

Elle sorted through the pile. "What about this one—*The Ice Princess?*"

"Why not?" laughed Emma. "It might be cool. And after all, we know how to handle them now!"

With, she smiled to herself, *a little help from EJ12.*

Emma Jacks and EJ12 return in

BOOK 2

JUMP START

Collect them all!